# BE NICE
## to Aunt Emma

## Anne Fine

Illustrated by
### Gareth Conway

Barrington Stoke

First published in 2021 in Great Britain by
Barrington Stoke Ltd
18 Walker Street, Edinburgh, EH3 7LP

www.barringtonstoke.co.uk

Text © 2021 Anne Fine
Illustrations © 2021 Gareth Conway

A CIP catalogue record for this book is available
from the British Library upon request

ISBN: 978-1-78112-965-4

Printed by Hussar Books, Poland

*For Johnny, who has himself accepted
the odd small bribe ...*

# Chapter 1

Dad said, "Be nice to Aunt Emma."

"Why?" I said. "Aunt Emma's never nice to me."

"Tansy, I'm sure she is," Dad said.

"I'm sure she's not," I said. "She's always telling me not to bang doors, and to hold my fork right, and stop kissing the dog, and—"

Dad didn't let me finish. "Yes, yes!" he said. "And she's spot on. You shouldn't kiss the dog."

"Anyone in the world," I said, "would rather kiss our dog than kiss Aunt Emma."

It's true, too! Cleo is very old and smelly. Her fur is dry and thin, and tufts of it are falling out. (She doesn't seem to mind.) She also farts a lot. Not very nice farts.

Still, I would rather hug and kiss Cleo any day than kiss Aunt Emma.

Aunt Emma is thirty-four. She is Mum's step-sister. We see her twice a year. She spends one night here on her way up to Scotland for her holiday, and one more on her way home.

The first time isn't so bad because I've half forgotten how horrible she can be. The second visit is terrible. I feel it coming for the whole ten days Aunt Emma is away. Part of me wants to put it off for ever, and part of me wants her to come back as soon as possible so that the misery will be over for another year.

I said to Dad, "Why does she have to stay here? Why can't she go to a hotel?"

"That isn't very nice," Dad said.

I said, "Nor is Aunt Emma," but Dad pretended that he hadn't heard.

# Chapter 2

Three Awful Things About Aunt Emma

1.  She never brings me a present.  She brings a
    bottle of wine for Mum, and a tin of coconut
    biscuits for Dad, and nothing at all for me.
    (I don't drink wine, and I hate coconut.)

2.  She drones on about the way she came.
    "I took the M25 and came off onto the M40.
    I stayed on that as far as Oxford.  Then I
    peeled off onto the A43 and joined the M1.
    I left that when I got to the M8 and then ...
    *blah, blah, blah, blah.*"

Like any of us *care?* I just wish that she'd get lost and not arrive at all.

3.   She sleeps in my bed, so I have to sleep on the blow-up mattress. I wouldn't mind the blow-up mattress if I was in my own room. In fact, I quite like it. But I have to move into Mum's office and keep to the rule that is written in big red letters on a notice over Mum's desk. It says:

*Please*

**I DON'T CARE HOW BORED YOU ARE.**

**DON'T YOU DARE TOUCH ANYTHING!**

**NOTHING AT ALL!**

**AND THIS MEANS YOU!**

*Thank you*

I know that it was Mum who pinned the notice on the wall. (And that it was Dad who added the only three polite words.) But when I have

to sleep under that notice, I always blame
Aunt Emma.

# Chapter 3

Aunt Emma came in just as I was starting on *Robot Race 3*. Before she'd even taken off her coat, I heard her say, "I see that Tansy's deep in one of her silly games, as usual."

As usual! I get one hour of screen time a day. One measly hour! And she has to choose that hour to come in and interrupt.

I gave her a look. So Dad gave me a look. "Now, Tansy. Say hello nicely to Aunt Emma," he warned me.

I nearly said, "*Hello-nicely-to-Aunt-Emma*," but stopped myself just in time.

Aunt Emma came across to peer at my screen. "Silly little green robots?" she said. "At your age? I would have thought that you'd have grown out of things like that years and years ago."

I expect there are more polite ways to say, "*Are you an idiot?*" But if there are, Aunt Emma didn't bother to think of one. Now she was staring at me.

"You've had your hair cut!" she told me (as if I didn't know). She made a bit of a face. "Oh, dear. I liked it much better the way it was before."

I don't know why she didn't go the whole way and say, "*Because, that way, it hid your ugly face better.*" Or, "*Did you do it yourself with the nail scissors?*"

Maybe she didn't say either of these things because she'd turned her fire on poor Cleo. "I see the Walking Smell Factory's still going strong," she said. "How *old* is this dog anyhow? A *hundred?*"

Whenever I complain about Aunt Emma, Mum tries to stick up for her. She says that, when her own mum married Emma's dad, she

and Emma hated sharing a room and said rude
things to one another all the time.  At first
it wasn't a game at all.  But later, when they
were friends, it turned into a joke, and nobody's
feelings were hurt.  (Well, half of it was a joke,
Mum says, and half of it was a left-over bad
habit.)

But things were very different in Dad's
family.  In his house, saying things like that was
never funny, it was just *rude.*  His mum had
even put a tiny poem up on the wall in a fancy
wooden frame.  She'd stitched the words in
rainbow colours:

*Always do, and always say,*
*The kindest thing in the nicest way.*

Dad says that, when he was a child, everyone
tried to be nice and polite to one another.
That's how he likes it, Dad says, and that is how
it's going to be in our house.

So I didn't dare say anything rude back to Aunt Emma, like, "Ooh! You're wearing an orange top with a purple skirt. Did you choose your colours for today in the pitch-dark?" Or, "That hat looks like a giant bogey." I just gave her the evil eye.

Dad helped me out. "Tansy, now that you've said hello nicely to Aunt Emma, why don't you go and have your screen time up in Mum's office?"

"Can I start my hour over again?" I asked him.

Nobody wants to start a fight in front of visitors, so Dad just gave a sigh and said, "Yes, Tansy. You can start the hour over."

# Chapter 4

Dad runs a petrol station, which is odd as he can't drive. (He got the job before his eyes went funny.) If things go wrong, then even if he's at home he has to go and sort them out. It happens quite a lot, and, sure enough, when I came down again ten minutes before supper, he was on the phone. There was a problem. One of the pumps had stuck.

Dad said, "I am so sorry, but I have to go and fix this. I hope it won't take long."

He phoned for a taxi, but they weren't answering.

"They're always busy on a Friday night," said Mum. "I'll run you over there and drop you off." She went to grab her car keys.

Dad put his hand on my arm and took me out of the room. "Be nice to Aunt Emma," he told me.

"Not that easy," I told him, "when she's so horrible to me. She's already said my hair looks like a haystack in a gale."

"She did not!" Dad told me.

"She nearly did," I said. "*And* she said that I was a screen addict. *And* that only a baby would want to play games that have robots in them."

"Nonsense!" said Dad.

"And she's told Cleo that she stinks."

"Nonsense," said Dad again. But he said it more weakly, because he'd heard Aunt Emma say it, so he knew that it was true.

Dad suddenly had an idea. "Listen, Tansy," he said. "What was that game you said you really, really, really wanted?"

I told him, "It's the next one. It's called *Robot Race 4*."

"OK," he said. "Be nice to Aunt Emma the whole time we're away, and I will buy it for you."

"Done deal!" I said.

That's when Mum called to him. "Tom, are you coming or not?"

"I'm coming!" Dad said. "Right this minute!"

And right that minute they were gone.

# Chapter 5

So there we were, me and Aunt Emma, left alone together. She gave me a look that sort of said, "*Oh, brilliant! Stuck with the brat!*" And I gave her a look that sort of said, "*Oh, wonderful! Stuck with the witch!*"

But I remembered about *Robot Race 4*, and I said sweetly, "Aunt Emma, can I make you a nice cup of tea while we wait for Mum and Dad to come back?"

"Why?" she said. "Do you plan to drop spiders in it?"

See?  Pretty nasty.  I began to see why Dad was so hot on people being nice and polite to one another.

I gave a tinkling laugh.  "No, no," I said.  "Just a nice cup of tea.  With maybe a biscuit or two to keep you going till we get our meal."

Aunt Emma said, "I get it!  You're pretending to be someone else!"

I wondered how long it had taken Dad to get Mum out of the habit of saying things like this.  But, *Robot Race 4!* I told myself. *Mine.  Very soon.  So long as I can keep my temper.*

"At least let me make you more comfy," I said, and pushed the little foot stool closer to her chair.

She looked at it as if it were a bomb about to explode.

Then I remembered what Dad always says when Old Mr Harper from next door comes round, so I said to Aunt Emma, "Are you sure you're warm enough? If you're cold, I could turn up the heating."

Aunt Emma gave me a killer stare. But I pressed on. "Or do you want me to fetch you a cushion? Or a rug for your knees?"

Aunt Emma snapped, "I'm not a hundred and four!"

And suddenly I realised that my being so polite was really, really, really annoying her.

Goody!

# Chapter 6

Mum rang to say that Dad had sorted out the problem with the pump. "He's just washing his hands," she said. "You two get started on supper, and we'll be back almost before you know it."

"Righty ho," I said.

I told Aunt Emma, "I have to dish up our supper."

Aunt Emma said, "Oh, aren't you the perfect Kitchen Princess?"

I nearly said, "*Better than being Queen of Mean!*" But then I thought of *Robot Race 4*. So I just gave Aunt Emma a twisted smile and put the big blue salad bowl on the table, along with the cheese tart and the baked potatoes. They were still warm.

I served Aunt Emma a slice of tart and offered her the big blue bowl. "Salad?"

She took a lot. (More than her fair share, anyway.)

I passed her the dish of baked potatoes. "Spud?"

She took the biggest.

"Butter?"

She took a lot of butter for just one potato.

I passed the salt towards her. "Salt?"

She shook her head.

I passed the pepper. "Pepper?"

"No, thanks!" she snapped, as if I was offering her a tub of broken glass to sprinkle on her plate. At first I thought she just didn't like pepper on her food. But then I realised that my good manners were getting on her nerves again.

Double goody! Because I knew I'd found a way to annoy Aunt Emma even more – and still get *Robot Race 4*.

I jumped to my feet and went to the cupboard where we keep all the jars and sauces and bottles.

I swung it open. "Ketchup?" I offered. "Brown sauce? Vinegar?"

She looked as if she was about to *growl*. So I moved to the fridge and opened that door.

"Salad dressing?" I offered cheerfully.  "Mustard? Pickle?"

Oh, I was making her *furious*. "Stop it!" she shouted at me. "You stop it, Tansy! Stop it right now! Be quiet and sit down!"

She can be pretty scary when she loses it. So I was quiet and sat down.

# Chapter 7

We heard a key in the door just then, and Mum and Dad came in. Mum said, "I'm glad you two got started with supper. Tom and I will soon catch up."

They sat down, and I passed the tart to Mum. Dad took his baked potato and put the other on Mum's plate. Mum served Dad with his slice of tart, and they both took some salad. And all the time that they were doing this, Aunt Emma glared at me across the table.

Mum and Dad were too busy to notice. But once Mum's plate was filled, she looked around the table. "Emma," she said, "You have your food. But would you like salt or pepper?"

I gave Aunt Emma a smug smile. She glared at me even more.

Mum saw the grumpy look on Aunt Emma's face. "Did you need something else?" she asked. "Do you want ketchup? Or brown sauce? Or vinegar?"

"Or salad dressing?" Dad said. "Maybe mustard? I think we even have pickle?"

Oh, you could tell that all this politeness was driving Aunt Emma crazy.

And that gave me an excellent idea.

I smiled at Aunt Emma across the table. "Did you come round the M25 today?" I asked.

Dad gave me a warm smile. I could tell he thought I was being really nice. But I didn't wait for an answer. I carried on. "Then maybe you came up the M40 as far as Oxford?"

Aunt Emma's scowl got worse. And Mum was watching me. But I carried on. "I expect you came off there onto the A43 to join the M1?"

By now Aunt Emma looked as cross as a bagful of starved cats, and even Dad was looking hard at me.

I didn't stop. "And maybe you came off the M1 at the M8 to get across to the A1?"

Dad stepped in. "Tansy, it's really nice of you to have remembered how Aunt Emma usually gets here. But now why don't you stop talking for a while and finish your lovely cheese tart and baked potato before they get cold?"

See?

*Always do, and always say,*
*The kindest thing in the nicest way.*

But he had got me to shut up.

# Chapter 8

Just as we finished eating, Dad's phone rang again. It was the garage, and the other pump had stuck.

"I have to go," he said. "So many people want to fill up on Friday night, ready for the weekend."

Mum gave me a worried look. And I was pretty worried, too! But then I thought of getting *Robot Race 4* and said as cheerfully as I could, "No problem! Aunt Emma and I will be just fine together!" I forced myself to give her a big smile. "Won't we, Aunt Emma?"

She had to smile too because Mum and Dad were watching. But I could tell those nice bright teeth would rather have been chewing stones than smiling at me.

Mum grabbed her keys, and she and Dad went out of the door again. I turned to look at Aunt Emma. The smile had frozen on her face. Now she was giving me a slit-eyed stare, as if she'd like to pull out my teeth and make a necklace with them.

I got quite scared, so just to stop her looking at me that way, I turned to the dishes stacked up next to the sink and said, "I think I'll start the washing up."

Aunt Emma sneered, "Oh, Little Miss Perfect!" And then, instead of saying she would help, she went into the other room.

I put my ear buds in to take a rest from her. After a bit, my favourite song came on. I must have started singing, because Aunt Emma came

back and tapped me on the arm. "Are you in *pain?*" she asked.

I took out my ear buds and told her, "No. I was just singing."

She gave me a nasty smile. "Not very musical, are you?" she said.

I lost it. Yes! I admit it! I suddenly lost it!

I snapped at her, "Better than being so bossy you'd argue with a signpost, and so aggressive you could start a fight in an empty room."

She stared at me. She just *stared*. And then she gave the most enormous smile. Not one of her pretend smiles with teeth like fangs. A real one. A proper, friendly smile that made you want to like her.

"Oh, good idea!" she said.

My turn to stare. "What? *What's* a good idea?"

"That we change sides."

I still didn't get it. "Change what sides?"

"You know," Aunt Emma said. "I'll be the crawly, polite one. And you can take my place and be the rude one."

# Chapter 9

I haven't had much practice in being rude. (It doesn't go down well with Dad.) But over the next hour I got really good at it. It can be *fun*.

When Aunt Emma asked me if I wanted half of her chocolate bar, I told her she had the brains of a cornflake and probably couldn't share out the feed for two hens. When she said in a very sweet way that one day I must come down to where she lived at Lee-on-Sea and stay with her, I said, "I don't know. Will two people fit under a rock?"

When she ran her hands through her hair to smooth it down, I asked if she had nits.

When she said she was getting a teensy bit worried about Mum and Dad being away so long, I said to her, "How old are you?  Six?"

Mum and Dad came back just as she was saying that I was really good company now, and I was about to say, "*Who am I, then? The New Leader of Freak Club?*" But luckily I stopped myself in time, so Mum and Dad only heard her bit!

Dad looked so pleased. "So Tansy's looked after you nicely, has she, Emma? I am so glad."

He gave me a smile and a wink, as if to say, "*Good job, Tansy. That robot game you want is almost in the bag.*"

I didn't want to blow it. I really wanted to get *Robot Race 4*. So I turned to Aunt Emma and asked her, "Now Mum and Dad are here, can we swap back the other way?"

"What other way?" Dad asked. "What were you playing, anyhow?"

I didn't dare answer, and Aunt Emma only grinned and said to me, "Yes, Tansy. Maybe swapping back is best. For now ..."

I stayed downstairs for only one more hour. Aunt Emma and I were alone for just a minute four times.

Four times!

The first time Mum and Dad were out of the room, she told me I talked as much nonsense as a Teletubby.

The second time, she called me Little Miss Biggity just because I told her that I wasn't bad at Maths.

The third time, when I told her I could juggle with two balls, she said she wouldn't believe it even if she saw it on CinemaScope with Dolby Digital Surround Sound.

The fourth time Mum and Dad were out of the room, she took the chance to say that, if a proper thought ever did cross my mind, it would have a very long and lonely journey.

By then I didn't think that I could keep it up, sticking at being nice to Aunt Emma whenever Mum or Dad was in the room. So I told them I was dead tired. I had to say goodnight politely, while Aunt Emma gave me a smug look. And by the time I got away safely to my blow-up bed under the sign in Mum's office, I was *worn out*.

# Chapter 10

I slept so well that I woke early next morning. I could hear Aunt Emma moving about in my bedroom, packing her bag again. So I tapped on the door.

"Can I come in and get some clean clothes?" I asked.

"Of course," she said. "And I want to thank you. You've been a sweetie, lending me your bed for the night."

I stared at her. I didn't know what to say.

She carried on. "And I think that you've made this room look perfectly charming. I love the posters on the wall, and all your little glass horses."

I was still staring.

Aunt Emma moved to the bookcase. "You've got so many books! Some of them look as if you've read them over and over again. I expect you're getting to be a really good reader. I bet all your teachers are proud of you. I know your mum and dad are."

She turned to smile at me. "How many is that?" she asked. "I've lost count. Is that three nice things that I've just said? Or is it four?"

I wasn't so amazed I couldn't count. "It was three," I said.

She nodded. "Oh, right," she said, and pointed. "You see that painting over there. Did you do that?"

"Yes," I said. "I did that in school, and Mum and Dad put it in a frame."

"It's beautiful," she said. "It's really good. You're a splendid artist." She folded her pyjamas and put them in her case.

"Right," she said. "So that's four nice things to make up for the four nasty things I said last night. We have to get even so we can play again when I come back."

"Play?" I said. "Is it a game?"

"Of course it's a game," she said. "Your mother and I used to play it all the time when we were growing up. Of course, she's out of the habit now."

"That's Dad," I said. "He can't stand people being rude."

"I know," she said. "But it's a shame. I miss the game. It was good fun. And seeing you always sets me off. You look so like your mum when we first had to share a room." She closed her case. "But your new way of playing it works even better. One nice. One nasty. And swapping sides. Brilliant!"

"I suppose it just felt a bit safer that way," I explained. "You can be very scary, you know. At one point last night your teeth looked like fangs. You almost *growled* at me."

She looked at her watch. "Well, last night there was a lot more time, so I could play the game properly. Right now, I'm rushing off. It's a long drive."

"I know!" I said. "I expect you'll be taking the A66 across to the M6, and then up the A74 as far as the M8, and then—"

Both of us burst out laughing. Then, "Shhh!" she said. "We mustn't wake your mum and dad. Just come downstairs and lock the door behind me."

I said, "I could make you some breakfast."

"It's very sweet of you," she said. "But I'd rather get on the road early. I'll see you next week anyway."

"Goody!" I said. (To my surprise, I wasn't even being nice and polite. I actually meant it.)

When she was on the doorstep, Aunt Emma turned to give me a peck on the cheek. "See you next week."

Beside me, Cleo let out the most enormous fart. She couldn't help it, but it was a stinker. Very, very smelly.

"Charming!" Aunt Emma said. "What a nice dog you have. That was the perfect goodbye!"

Both of us burst out laughing.

*

When Dad got up, he said, "Has Emma gone? I hoped she'd stay for breakfast."

I told him, "I did offer to make her some."

Dad told me, "That was nice of you. And you were an angel, Tansy, all through her visit. Well done."

"I get my *Robot Race 4*, then?"

He grinned at me. "Oh, yes, you get your game. But don't for a moment think that getting a treat is going to happen every time Aunt Emma visits."

"Oh, that's OK," I said. "I think that I won't need it next time."

Our books are tested
for children and young people by
children and young people.

Thanks to everyone who consulted on
a manuscript for their time and effort in
helping us to make our books better
for our readers.

More from
**Anne Fine**

A
**Remarkable
Ear**

Illustrated by
Roxana de Rond

**Anne
Fine**

978-1-78112-944-9

A musical story of patience,
practice and courage!

# More from Anne Fine

Anne Fine

Tales from WEIRD STREET

Anne Fine

back on WEIRD STREET

978-1-78112-572-4

978-1-78112-788-9

# Creepy tales full of chills and thrills!